Dear Parent:
Your child's love of reading starts here!

Every child learns to read in a different way and at his or her own speed. Some go back and forth between reading levels and read favorite books again and again. Others read through each level in order. You can help your young reader improve and become more confident by encouraging his or her own interests and abilities. From books your child reads with you to the first books he or she reads alone, there are I Can Read Books for every stage of reading:

SHARED READING
Basic language, word repetition, and whimsical illustrations, ideal for sharing with your emergent reader

BEGINNING READING
Short sentences, familiar words, and simple concepts for children eager to read on their own

READING WITH HELP
Engaging stories, longer sentences, and language play for developing readers

READING ALONE
Complex plots, challenging vocabulary, and high-interest topics for the independent reader

ADVANCED READING
Short paragraphs, chapters, and exciting themes for the perfect bridge to chapter books

I Can Read Books have introduced children to the joy of reading since 1957. Featuring award-winning authors and illustrators and a fabulous cast of beloved characters, I Can Read Books set the standard for beginning readers.

A lifetime of discovery begins with the magical words "I Can Read!"

Visit www.icanread.com for information
on enriching your child's reading experience.

For Leah
—L.M.S.

For Arthur, Nora, Harry, and Ethan
—S.K.H.

Mittens, Where Is Max? Text copyright © 2011 by Lola M. Schaefer Illustrations copyright © 2011 by Susan Kathleen Hartung
All rights reserved. Manufactured in China. No part of this book may be used or reproduced in any manner whatsoever without written
permission except in the case of brief quotations embodied in critical articles and reviews. For information address HarperCollins
Children's Books, a division of HarperCollins Publishers, 10 East 53rd Street, New York, NY 10022.
www.icanread.com

Library of Congress Cataloging-in-Publication Data is available.
ISBN 978-0-06-170227-3 (trade bdg.) — ISBN 978-0-06-170226-6 (pbk.)

11 12 13 14 15   SCP   10 9 8 7 6 5 4 3 2 1   ❖   First Edition

I Can Read!™ SHARED READING My First

Mittens, Where Is Max?

story by **Lola M. Schaefer**

pictures by **Susan Kathleen Hartung**

HARPER
An Imprint of HarperCollinsPublishers

Mittens wants to play.

He rolls his toy.

Squeak.

Squeak.

Squeak.

Plop!

The toy is no fun.
Mittens wants to play.
He wants to play
with his friend Max.

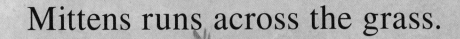

Mittens runs across the grass.

He crawls under the fence.

This is where Max lives.
But where is Max?

But Max is not here.

Where is Max?

Mittens runs to the back steps.

This is where Max eats.

But Max is not here.
Where is Max?

Mittens calls Max.

"MEOW."

But Max does not come.

Where is Max?

15

Squeak. Squeak.

Mittens hears his toy.

He sees his toy.

It is rolling, rolling, rolling.

Squeak.

Squeak.

Squeak.

Mittens crawls under
the fence.
Look who's here!

It's Max.

Max was looking for Mittens.

He wanted to play, too.

This is where Mittens
and Max play!